LARK and the
DIAMOND CAPER

NATASHA DEEN

Illustrated by MARCUS CUTLER

orca Echoes

ORCA BOOK PUBLISHERS

Library and Archives Canada Cataloguing in Publication

Deen, Natasha, author
Lark and the diamond caper / Natasha Deen ; illustrated by Marcus Cutler.
(Orca echoes)

Issued in print and electronic formats.
ISBN 978-1-4598-1400-4 (softcover).—ISBN 978-1-4598-1401-1 (pdf).—
ISBN 978-1-4598-1402-8 (epub)

I. Cutler, Marcus, illustrator II. Title. III. Series: Orca echoes
PS8607.E444L35 2017   jc813'.6   c2017-900817-x
c2016-900818-8

First published in the United States, 2017
Library of Congress Control Number: 2017933030

Summary: In this early chapter book, Lark and her brother, Connor, find the culprit when a
pair of diamond earrings goes missing from the general store.

Orca Book Publishers gratefully acknowledges the support for its publishing programs
provided by the following agencies: the Government of Canada through the Canada Book Fund
and the Canada Council for the Arts, and the Province of British Columbia
through the BC Arts Council and the Book Publishing Tax Credit.

Edited by Liz Kemp
Cover artwork and interior illustrations by Marcus Cutler
Author photo by Curtis Comeau

ORCA BOOK PUBLISHERS
www.orcabook.com

Printed and bound in Canada.

20 19 18 17 • 4 3 2 1

For Alida

Chapter One

My name is Lark Ba, and I have butterflies in my stomach. Not really. That would be awful for the butterflies. And it wouldn't be much fun for me either. Butterflies in my stomach is something my *halmoni*—that's Korean for *grandmother*—says. It means I'm really excited or ~~nervus nerevhus~~ nervous. Right now, I am both.

Yesterday my brother, Connor, and me solved our very first mystery!

Which was amazing, because Connor is my younger brother. I'm older by ten whole minutes, which is a lot of minutes, and I didn't think he would be such a great big help.

Our case was the bestest. The librarian, Mrs. Robinson, had lost the key to the library. We found it. That made us investigators, which made me *so* happy. Especially because investigator ~~rimes ryms~~ rhymes with alligator, and I love those.

Today was going to be an even better, more exciting day. Today Connor and I were going to solve another mystery. I was excited because I didn't know what kind of mystery it would be. But that wasn't why I had butterflies in my stomach. I had butterflies in my stomach because Connor and I had to practice our magic trick for our family talent night.

Family talent night is about learning to do something ~~unyoushal~~ ~~unujual~~ unusual or cool. Dad calls it *everyday magic*. Once a month, Mom and Dad decorate our living room with colored lights and put on old-folks' music. Then we have a contest to see who can perform the coolest trick. Last month Dad won, because he fit thirty cheese crackers in his mouth. The time before, Mom won for making a hula hoop spin around her waist for a million years! Okay, maybe not that long, but it was a long time! Connor and I are determined to win this family talent night. We are going to practice and practice and practice until we are the bestest.

At least, we were going to practice as soon as we figured out what trick to do. "I think I should saw you in half," I said. "That would be a great trick."

"No way." Connor shook his head. "You're clumsy and klutzy and—"

"I am not."

"You are so. I don't think you should have a saw or anything sharp in your hands. Ever."

I sighed. "But it would be so cool."

"I could saw you in half," he said.

"You're too little to do that."

"I am not!"

I decided to ignore him. We had important ~~desishuns~~ ~~deesixtions~~ decisions to make. We could argue later. "What about if we turn Max into a rabbit?" I asked. "We could dress him up in a top hat and a red cape."

Max is our dog. He was sleeping beside Connor on the couch. He lifted his head when I said his name. I rubbed his ears and said, "You'd make a great assistant.

We'd just have to get Mom and Dad to get us a rabbit."

"Hmm," said Connor. "Max doesn't like it when we make him wear his winter coat. He won't like the cape. And I think he'll try to eat the hat. Plus, I don't think Mom and Dad will get us a rabbit."

"Those are good points. Finding a really great idea for the magic trick is tougher than I thought."

"You know what would be a great trick? Making you disappear," said Connor.

"Ha-ha."

"But you know what would be an even greater trick?" he asked. "Making you be quiet. Mom and Dad and Halmoni will never believe it if we do that trick!"

"I can be quiet!"

"No you can't. You talk a lot!"

I took a breath and decided to be patient. After all, I was his big sister. "We need a good trick. And remember, I'm the magician. You are the assistant."

"Only for the first time we do the trick," he said. "But when we do it again, I get to be the magician."

"Neither of us will get to be a magician if we can't come up with a trick."

Connor closed his eyes. "I still like the idea of making something disappear, even if it can't be Max or an annoying sister—"

"I'm not annoying, and I'm your *big* sister—"

"Twin sister."

"I'm older."

"Argh! By ten minutes!" Connor said.

"I'm still older." I patted his hand. "But when we grow up, I'll let you be taller. So we both win."

He thought about that for a minute. "Okay, that's a good deal."

I jumped off the couch and went to the bookshelf. We'd just been to the library and borrowed a stack of books.

Some of them were about detectives. Some were about astronauts. Some were about magic. The night before, I'd read a super-great book about a P.I. who wore a cool hat and squinted when he talked. "Here." I gave Connor two books on magic tricks, and I took two books. "Let's look through these for ideas."

I have *d-y-s-l-e-x-i-a*. Dyslexia. It means that when I read, numbers and letters jump and swim on the page. I have a special piece of see-though paper to help me. It's red—my favorite color. And when I read, I put it over the page. Changing the color of the paper can make the words behave. We sat and flipped through the pages. "Oh! I like this one!" I turned the book around so Connor could see the pages. "We can make a coin go through the coffee table!"

"Really?" He put down his book and came over. "Cool. How do we do it?"

"We need a fork, a knife, a napkin and two quarters," I said. "Oh, and a table."

He rolled his eyes. "No kidding."

I sighed.

"Let's go to the kitchen," he said. "That's where we'll find most of those things."

Connor, Max and I went to the kitchen. I gave Max a doggy treat, and Connor gave him some water.

"I'll get the knife," said Connor. "You shouldn't be around anything sharp."

I took a deep breath and practiced my patience.

Then I went to the drawer and brought out two coins from the spare-change jar.

Connor walked to another drawer and took out a knife and fork.

"Okay," I said. "Napkins." They were in a high ~~cupbored~~ ~~cuboared~~ cupboard. We'd need a chair. Connor helped me take a chair over to the cupboard.

"You hold it steady," I said. "I'll get the napkins."

"Are you sure? You're kind of clumsy."

"Connor!" I took a deep breath and reminded myself I'm a patient big sister. "You are stronger than me, so you hold it, okay?"

"Okay." He smiled.

I smiled back. Then I climbed up on the chair and reached for the napkins. Only they were higher than my fingers, so I went up on my tiptoes.

"Are you sure I shouldn't do it?" Connor asked

"I almost have it." I reached and reached and reached. I couldn't touch the napkins, but I *could* touch the plastic plate they were on. I grabbed it and pulled. Only I pulled kind of hard, and the plate went flying out of my hand!

It flew through the air, hit the fridge and smashed on the floor with a big *crash*!

Uh-oh. That was sure to wake Mom and Dad. They were going to be grumpy. We heard a bedroom door open. I looked at Connor. He looked at me. *Gulp*.

Chapter Two

Lucky for us, it was Halmoni. She's never grumpy with us. Not even with Connor. Which is really amazing, because Connor can be *really* annoying.

"I heard some noise," she said. "What's going on?"

"We were trying to get supplies for our magic trick," I said.

"For the family talent night? How exciting! What trick are you going to do?" she asked.

"We're going to make a coin go through one end of a table and come out on the other side!"

"My goodness," she said. "That sounds like an amazing trick!"

"We need a napkin for it," I told her. "That's when the crash happened. I dropped a plate."

"Well, it looks like you have the napkins now," she said. "So why don't we practice?"

We sat at the table. I put the fork and knife on the napkin just like the book showed us. "That holds the napkin in place."

"Now what?" asked Halmoni.

Connor looked at the page. "Put one quarter on the table. Make sure it lies flat. Then put your index finger on the top and your thumb on the bottom of the coin."

I did what Connor said.

"Now bring your fingers together. Do it really fast, so the quarter will slide under the napkin."

I tried, but pinching a quarter was a lot harder than it looked. After a bunch of attempts, my fingers were sore. "Connor, you try."

He did, and he did a better job, but it was still really hard.

"Halmoni, do you want to try?"

"I would love to." She held the edges of the quarter in her hand, then pinched! The quarter disappeared under the napkin. Almost. "Goodness," she said. "This is tricky!"

We practiced and practiced—until we heard Mom and Dad's bedroom door open.

"Uh-oh!" Halmoni scooped the coins into her pocket and picked up the knife and fork. "We don't want them to see what we're doing until we can wow them with your trick!"

I took the fork and knife from Halmoni and put them away.

"Practicing magic tricks is hard work," she said. "Connor, take these napkins and set the table, please. Let's have some banana pancakes with cinnamon and icing sugar for breakfast."

Delicious!

"Lark, the recipe is in the recipe binder," said Halmoni. "Can you please find it and walk me through it?"

"No problem!" I ran and got my red paper. Then I came back and looked through the binder. When I found the recipe, I read the ~~instrukshun~~ ~~insertshuckhn~~ instructions to Halmoni.

Connor helped her measure and mix the ~~ingreedients engredients~~ ingredients.

Pretty soon we had a giant heap of pancakes. And they smelled so good! All sweet and spicy. "We have a big day of magic-trick practicing and mystery solving," I announced. "I should have lots of pancakes."

"Me too," said Connor. "I might have to lift something heavy."

I had four fluffy, yummy pancakes. So did Connor. When we finished eating, we helped Halmoni clean up.

"What shall we do while we're waiting for Mom and Dad to leave for work?" asked Halmoni.

"I know!" I said. "I bet lots of people heard how we solved the case of the lost library key yesterday. We should see if there are any new cases."

Connor nodded. "We were awesome. I bet Mrs. Robinson told everyone who came into the library, and I bet those people told other people."

"I agree," said Halmoni. "I bet everyone sang your praises."

Connor looked confused. "Why would people sing about us?"

Halmoni laughed. "It means you did such a good job that everyone's talking about you! When people talk about you in a good way, it's called praise. And when they do lots of talking, it's called *singing your praises*."

"Oh, I get it." Connor nodded.

"We should check and see if anyone else needs help to solve a mystery," I said.

"Great idea," said Halmoni. "Let's start with the mailbox. After that we can check our emails."

We ran outside and looked in the mailbox. Nothing.

"Time to check the emails and solve a case!" said Connor.

We ran back inside. Today was going to be the bestest day ever!

Chapter Three

Halmoni sat at the computer. Connor was on one side of her. I was on the other.

"Let's check my email first," said Halmoni. She opened her email program. She looked through her messages. There was one from our aunt and one from our uncle and one from our *babu*—that's Swahili for *grandfather*. But there were no emails asking for help from Connor and me.

"How about if I check the one your mom, dad, babu and I share?" Halmoni checked that one too. There were no messages asking for our help.

"Wow," I said. "Nothing at all."

"We should stay optimistic," said Connor.

I nodded. I like that word. It's a grown-up way of saying, "Stay positive."

"Maybe they sent it to my other address." Halmoni checked. There was a message from one of her clients and a bunch from her friends. But there were no messages for us.

I gave Connor my big-sister smile. "It'll be okay."

He nodded, but his shoulders were all droopy.

"No emails from anyone," said Halmoni. "That's great news!"

Great news? Connor and I looked at each other. What was Halmoni thinking?

"Great news?" asked Connor. "What do you mean?"

"It's great news," said Halmoni, "because now you get to go out and find work!"

"I don't understand," said Connor.

I didn't either.

Halmoni grinned. "It's fantastic because now we can make posters. We can tell the whole world about your being private investigators. It's much more fun than sitting and waiting for a case to come your way."

I really liked this idea, and Halmoni's plan. It made me think of a word, but I couldn't remember it. It started with a *p*, and it had an *o* in it, and it was a good word.

She stood. "Come on. We need to be on the ball for this! I'm going to get our craft box."

When Halmoni left the kitchen, Connor turned to me. His face had lots of worried squiggles. "I don't know if I can be on a ball," he said.

"Me either," I said. "Cutting paper and drawing might be hard if we have to sit on Mom and Dad's yoga balls to do it." I stopped and had a good think. "Maybe Halmoni can be on the ball, and we can be on the chairs."

Connor nodded. "I think that's a good idea."

Halmoni came back with our giant blue craft box. It was full of paper and markers and glue and glitter. We sat around the table. Halmoni didn't say anything about being on the ball. I decided not to remind her.

I am really good at drawing. So I made an alligator holding a magnifying glass. Connor is really good at printing. Above the alligator, he wrote, *Lark and Connor Ba, Private Investigators. Cases solved for $1. No mystery too big or too small.*

We made a bunch of posters.

"These look great!" said Halmoni when we had finished. "It's still early. Let's walk around. We can put the posters in our neighbors' mailboxes."

She paused and looked at each of us. "Quietly. We'll do it *quietly*. It's still very early." She gave me an extra-hard look. "Quiet. Got it?"

I nodded. I knew exactly why she'd looked at me extra hard. She wanted to make sure *I* made sure Connor behaved.

It took a long time, but we *quietly* put a poster in every mailbox.

"It's ten o'clock. You know what we should do?" asked Halmoni.

"Get ice cream?" I said.

"It's a little early for that," said Halmoni.

"But we've been working really hard," Connor told her.

"And ice cream is made of milk," I added. "And that's one of the five food groups."

Halmoni made a gurgley-coughy sound, and it looked like she was trying to hide a smile.

"I bet a milkshake would help that cough," I said.

"I was thinking we should go the post office and put up one of the posters on the bulletin board," said Halmoni.

"That's a good idea." Connor nodded. "We'll get the ice cream after."

The post office was inside the general store. The general store is owned by Mr. and Mrs. Lee. The store sells groceries and medicine. It has a coffee shop with

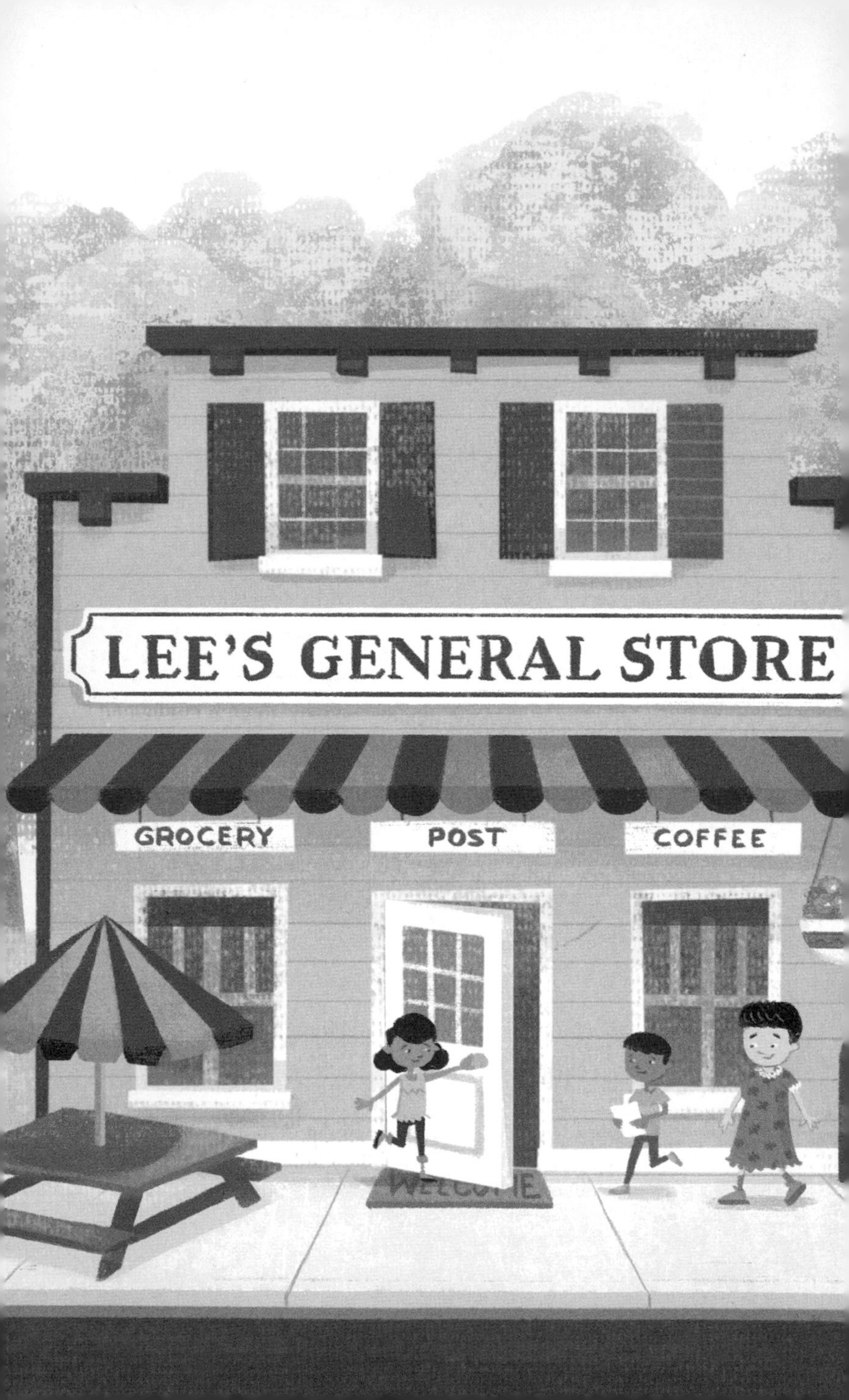
LEE'S GENERAL STORE
GROCERY
POST
COFFEE
WELCOME

~~delishush~~ ~~deelishus~~ delicious hot chocolate and cookies. Plus, it has a giant tank with lots and lots of colorful fish.

When Mr. and Mrs. Lee opened the store, they asked Dad to set up the fish tank because he works at the aquarium. And Dad let Connor and me help. We picked out a big rectangular tank and put lots of fun stuff inside. Pebbles, treasure chests and scuba divers. Then we got to pick out the fish. We chose African cichlids, tetras, and guppies. I love going to the general store to look at the fish. It's like watching a swimming rainbow, and it always makes me happy.

"We can see the fish," said Connor. "That will be cool."

I nodded. "It's too bad we aren't getting there earlier. We could have helped Mr. Lee feed them."

"I know," Connor replied. "But they always get their food at eight."

I opened the door for Halmoni and let Connor go ahead of me. Then I went inside, and I did not like what I saw, not one bit. Nope, nope, nope.

Chapter Four

A bunch of grown-ups stood by the cash register, and they all looked grumpy. Really, *really* grumpy.

"What's going on? What happened?" asked Halmoni.

"We've had a theft!" said Mrs. Lee. Usually, Mrs. Lee looks neat and tidy. She likes to wear her black hair in a bun and keep her apron bright white and clean. Right now she didn't look like that at all. Her bun was lopsided, and pieces of her hair were loose. Her shirt was all crumpled, and her apron was covered in dirt.

I grabbed Connor's arm and whispered, "This is so great! It's a case!" I stepped forward into the group of grown-ups. "Mrs. Lee, Connor and I are private investigators. Can you tell us what happened? Maybe we can help."

"Oh, Lark, Connor, that's very sweet of you to offer." She tried to push her hair back into place, but it wouldn't stay. "It's a big theft, though, and I think we should wait for the police."

"I don't know why I have to be here," Mrs. Wiedman interrupted. "I didn't steal anything."

"Me either," said Mrs. Paradowski. "And I don't like being accused of stealing."

"Everyone must stay here until the police arrive!" Mrs. Lee said in a stern voice. "They will want to question everyone!"

"I can't believe it," Henry said glumly. He worked for the Lees. "I came into work today because I needed the extra money to fix my car. Now I'm a robbery suspect!"

"How do you think I feel?" asked Mrs. Weidman. "I only came in because I needed milk and bread!"

"Bad news," said Mr. Lee as he put down his phone. "There was construction on the highway, and some drivers got into an accident. Officer Duong won't be able to come for a couple of hours." He took off his glasses and rubbed his eyes. "This is terrible."

"You should tell us what happened," said Connor. "We really can help."

Mr. Lee sank onto the bench that was beside the front door. "That's very kind, but this is a matter for the grown-ups."

"But—" said Connor.

I put my finger to my mouth and shushed him.

"Why are you telling me to be quiet?" he asked.

I pulled Connor away from the grown-ups. "I learned about this from my book yesterday. If we're quiet, we'll get the information we need. The detective in the story called it *spilling the beans*. He said people can't help but talk about a crime. Especially suspects."

"What's are suspects?"

"They're the people who might have committed the crime. They're called suspects. Then whoever did the bad thing is called the culprit."

"Oh, that makes sense." Connor thought for a minute. "So does your idea of listening quietly." He looked at me. "Can you be quiet?"

"It'll be my best magic trick."

He nodded.

This was exciting—and kind of scary. The butterflies were in my stomach *and* my throat! We were about to investigate our second case!

Chapter Five

"This is all so terrible," said Mrs. Lee to Halmoni. "Our niece is a jewelry maker, and today we got the first shipment of her necklaces and earrings. And someone stole a pair of earrings! Diamond earrings!"

Mr. Lee shook his head and walked over to them. "I can't believe it. I just can't believe it." He looked around the room. "Sung and Henry have worked for us for a long time. Mrs. Wiedman and Mrs. Paradowski have been our clients for an even longer time! I can't believe any of them would steal from us."

I felt bad for the Lees. They were nice people, and they didn't deserve to have their things stolen. I felt bad for the rest of the group too. Only one of them had stolen the jewelry. It wasn't fair that they were all suspects. It was up to Connor and me to figure out the truth. The grown-ups didn't want to talk to us, but there was someone who would help.

I went to Halmoni and whispered, "We need some information."

"What kind?" she whispered back.

I squinted, just like the detective in the story I'd read, and said, "We need to know what happened before the robbery.

We might be able to figure out who the suspect is."

She nodded and said to Mrs. Lee, "Can you tell me exactly what happened? Start at the beginning, please. Where was everyone standing?"

"Mrs. Wiedman and Henry were by the fish tank," said Mrs. Lee.

"We were watching them swim," said Henry.

"Mrs. Paradowski and I were over there." Mrs. Lee pointed at a spot beside the tank. "We were looking at the jewelry," she said.

"Sung and I were at the cash register," said Mr. Lee.

"A bunch of kids came in," said Mrs. Lee, "and they seemed to be fighting with each other."

Connor leaned in. "Three guesses who that was," he said to me. "Sophie and her friends."

"It might not be—"

"It was Sophie and her friends," continued Mrs. Lee.

Connor nodded. "I'm not surprised."

"I went over to see what was going on," said Mrs. Lee. "It turned out they weren't arguing. They were just talking loudly. And they were doing a science experiment, I think." She paused. "They needed a special kind of mints, and a specific type of soda. I went back to help Mrs. Paradowski, and the kids went to the soda and candy aisle."

I looked at Connor.

He looked at me.

We both knew what kind of experiment Sophie and her friends

were doing. More on that later. "What happened next?"

"I went to get some milk," said Mrs. Wiedman. "I couldn't see what was going on."

That made sense. The fish tank was in the middle of the store, and the jewelry was on a table beside it. The milk was kept at the back. Mrs. Wiedman wouldn't have seen anything because she would have walked away from the display.

"I couldn't see anything either," said Henry, "because I went to help Mrs. Wiedman."

"After he fed the fish," said Mrs. Wiedman.

He nodded. "They looked hungry."

"Sophie and her friends took the mints and soda to the cash register," said Mr. Lee. "I rang in their purchases, and Sung packed everything into their shopping bag. Then they left."

"I chose a necklace I liked and went to the cash register, and I paid for my things," said Mrs. Paradowski.

Sung nodded. "That's true. I have the receipt here in the cash register."

I looked over at Connor. "This is kind of confusing. There are a lot of people to keep track of."

Connor nodded. He flipped over one of our posters. "Let's write this down." At the top of the page he wrote:

BEFORE THE THEFT. Underneath that he wrote:

Mrs. Weidman and Henry stood by the fish.

Mrs. Lee and Mrs. Paradowski stood by the jewelry table.

Mr. Lee and Sung stood by the cash register.

Sophie and her friends went to the soda and candy aisle.

Then he wrote, **DURING THE THEFT.** Underneath that he wrote:

Mrs. Weidman and Henry went to get milk.

Sophie and her friends paid for their soda and mints and left.

Mrs. Lee helped Mrs. Paradowski choose some jewelry. Then they walked to the cash register.

Mr. Lee and Sung remained by the cash register.

I patted Connor on the shoulder. "That's good. A great P.I. keeps track of everything." I turned to Mrs. Lee. "What happened next?"

"I went to leave," said Mrs. Paradowski.

"I went to pay for my milk—" said Mrs. Wiedman.

"But then you remembered you needed bread," added Henry. "I know because I went with you to help. The bakery section isn't anywhere near the jewelry section."

"I went to tidy up the jewelry display," said Mrs. Lee. "That's when I noticed an empty spot. Someone had stolen the earrings!"

Chapter Six

"Is it possible they just fell on the floor?" asked Connor.

I shushed him. We were supposed to be quiet and listening. But I guess the grown-ups were focused on the mystery, because Mr. Lee said, "We searched everywhere."

"Mrs. Paradowski and I emptied my purse to prove I didn't have anything," said Mrs. Wiedman to Halmoni.

"We feel terrible about it." Mrs. Lee squeezed Mrs. Wiedman's hand. "But someone must have taken them."

"But no one here has the earrings," said Mr. Lee.

I looked at Halmoni. We needed to check the bags and pockets, but I didn't want to interrupt the grown-ups.

"Hmm," said Halmoni. "I wonder if the earrings just fell and got caught in someone's clothes." She smiled at Connor and me. "You two are smaller than us. Maybe if the earrings fell on the floor and rolled into a corner, you might find them."

"Do you mind if we triple-check?" I asked Mrs. Lee. "May we look around the store?"

"I suppose it wouldn't hurt," said Mrs. Lee.

"If we're looking again, I might as well go through my purse once more," said Mrs. Paradowski.

"Mine too," said Mrs. Wiedman.

We watched as everyone checked their stuff. Henry emptied his pockets, and so did Sung. Mrs. Wiedman and Mrs. Paradowski took everything out of their bags. Even the Lees emptied their pockets.

No earrings.

Connor put down his pen and paper. We went to the jewelry display. We lifted each piece of jewelry and looked under it. Then we looked under the box. And then under the table. There was no pair of diamond earrings.

Next, we looked around the fish tank. In front of it. Behind it. Under it. Still no diamond earrings. We kept

looking and looking and looking. But those earrings were playing the bestest game of hide-and-seek.

Connor made a frowny face. "These earrings weren't just stolen. Someone made them disappear. But no one has left the store. We have a mystery, Lark, but it's a big one. First we have to figure out who stole the earrings. But then we have to figure out how the culprit made them disappear."

I stood and thought. Then thought some more. "Someone did leave the store. Sophie."

"Aw." Connor's forehead went wrinkly. "I know she's a pain, but do you think she'd really steal from the Lees?"

"No," I said, "and I don't think her friends did either. But maybe the earrings got snagged on a sweater or fell in the shopping bag."

"I guess." Connor put the paper and pen in his pocket. "Let's go and talk to her."

Halmoni walked us to the door and whispered, "I'll stay here and listen. Maybe someone will give something away."

"That's good thinking," said Connor. "You're an excellent assistant."

Halmoni covered her face and coughed.

I nodded, then put my hand on her arm. "You should drink some orange juice to help with your cough."

She nodded solemnly. "That's a very good idea."

"Keep your ears open and see if anyone spills the beans," I said.

"Yes, Halmoni, listen hard. See if anyone spills the beans, carrots or peas."

Halmoni made that gurgley-coughy sound and nodded.

Chapter Seven

We walked a few blocks over to Sophie's house and rang the doorbell. There was no answer. I was going to knock when Connor tapped my arm.

"Do you hear that?"

It sounded like a tire or a balloon losing air. "It's coming from the backyard."

"Let's go and see."

We followed the noise and found Sophie and our other friends, Franklin and Kate, behind the house. They were standing by a pile of soda bottles and didn't notice us.

"We're going to need more soda," I heard Sophie say. "We need more fizz. It's got to be spectacular for our movie!"

"Movie?" Connor asked.

Everyone turned to look at us.

"Hey! Connor and Lark!" Kate ran over to us. "Yeah, we're making a monster movie."

"But what are the soda and mints for?" asked Connor.

"Because," I said, "if you put one of the mints into a two-liter bottle of soda, it makes a great explosion!"

Connor rolled his eyes. "I know what happens if you mix soda and mints. I meant, what does an explosion have to do with a monster movie?"

"The monster is born in a volcano," said Franklin, "and when he comes out of the volcano, there's a huge eruption!"

"Cool!" Connor said. "Can I help? I'm great with this kind of stuff."

Grrr. Little brothers. "Maybe you can help them after we solve our case."

"Oh." He slapped his forehead with his hand. "Right."

"You've got a case?" asked Sophie. "I thought you had solved it. Didn't you already find the library key, baa baa Lark sheep?"

The smile disappeared from Connor's face. "That's not funny."

"Sure it is," I said. "Because our last name is Ba, and that's the same sound sheep make."

"Still not funny," said Connor.

Sometimes Connor can't take a joke, but I knew Sophie was joking. She and I are best friends—she just doesn't know it yet. But friendship and explaining jokes would have to wait. I had a case to solve.

"You went to the general store earlier," I said.

Kate, Franklin and Sophie nodded.

"Someone stole a pair of earrings," said Connor.

Franklin shook his head and took a step back. "It wasn't me!"

"Me either," said Kate.

"We don't think you stole anything. But maybe you saw something?"

Franklin shook his head again. "I'm sorry. My job was to get the soda. When we went into the store, that's all I was looking for."

"My job was to get the mints," said Kate. "I didn't see anything either."

"What about you, Sophie?" asked Connor.

"I was too busy planning the movie. And I'm still busy planning the movie. I don't have time to help with anything." She put an empty bottle into a recycling bag.

"You must have noticed something," said Connor.

"What I noticed is that our explosions aren't cool enough for the movie. And I notice you're wasting my time. I can't help."

"You're really good at noticing stuff," I said. "If you help me, I can help you make the explosion really, extremely, superduper, totally cool."

Sophie stopped loading the recycling bag. "Promise?"

I nodded.

So did Connor.

"Okay, I'll help."

Connor took out the paper with his notes and showed Sophie.

She read it. "Yes, that looks right."

"Exactly right?" I asked.

Sophie gave the paper back to Connor. "Exactly right." She gave me a worried look. "Are you still going to help with the monster movie? Even though I didn't add anything?"

I nodded. "You helped. So will I. After I solve the—"

Connor elbowed me.

"After *we* solve the case."

I smiled and waved goodbye, but inside I didn't feel very smiley. I had hoped Sophie would give me a clue, but I was still stuck. Who had stolen the earrings, and how did they make the jewelry disappear?

"We should go back to the store," said Connor, "and take another look. Maybe we missed something. Or maybe Halmoni's found another clue to the culprit."

I nodded.

Connor gave me a smile and patted me on the shoulder. "It's going to be fine. We'll solve this."

That made me feel better. "You're a really good little brother."

Connor sighed. "I just thought of a new magic trick."

"Really? What?"

"Making you realize we're twins, and you're not older."

Now it was my turn to sigh. Little brothers can be so much work.

Chapter Eight

When we got back to the store, Halmoni came up to us.

"Were Sophie and her friends helpful?"

I shook my head.

So did Connor.

"That's okay," said Halmoni. "We'll figure it out."

Mrs. Lee came over. "Thank you for trying to help. I'm sorry you didn't find out anything new." She gave us a big smile. "The good news is that Officer Duong will be here in ten minutes." Mrs. Lee leaned in. "And we're going to give you a box of Creamsicles as thanks for trying to help."

"Thank you, Mrs. Lee," said Connor.

She smiled and walked away.

This was no good, no good at all. If we didn't solve the case in the next ten minutes, the police would take over! Suddenly my bestest day had turned into my worstest day.

"We have to find out the solution," Connor said to me. "If we don't, no one will ever hire us!" His face was super wrinkly.

"It'll be okay," I said. "We'll figure this out." I didn't know if that was true, but I didn't want him to feel bad.

"Do you think so?"

I nodded. "Yep, yep, you don't have to be—" I couldn't remember the word, but it was a good one, and it had a great *oo* sound. It meant when you were so sad it was like rain clouds were over your head.

"Let's take a closer look at the display case," I suggested. We went over to it, and I tried *really* hard to think like the P.I. in the book. I looked at all the jewelry. There were red stones and blue, some that were black, some were clear, and some that were green.

"There is a lot of stuff here," said Connor. "Earrings and necklaces and bracelets." He stared at each of them. "If I was a thief, I'd steal earrings because they're the easiest to hide." His face went all frowny. "But why would I steal diamonds?"

"Because," Halmoni said as she came to stand by us, "they are the most valuable."

"Oh." He nodded. "Okay."

"Connor, I think you have a very good idea," I said. "We should each pretend to be the thief. Maybe then we can figure out who it is."

"We have four suspects." He took his notebook out. "Mrs. Lee, Mrs. Weidman, Henry and Mrs. Paradowski. They were all by the jewelry case."

"Henry and Mrs. Weidman were by the fish tank, looking at the fish," said Halmoni.

"Does that mean we only have two suspects?" Connor looked at me. "I can't imagine Mrs. Lee would steal from her niece." He shook his head. "But I can't imagine any of them would steal."

"Me either," I said.

I closed my eyes and thought hard. I pretended I was the thief. I used my imagination to pretend I'd stolen some earrings and then something happened that made me worry I was going to get caught. So I had to hide them. I had to put the earrings somewhere I would find them later where no one else would see them.

I thought and thought and thought.

"I'm excited about getting a box of Creamsicles. It's been forever since we had the pancakes, and I'm really hungry," I heard Connor say to Halmoni. "But they won't taste as good if we don't solve the robbery."

I was getting hungry too. I bet we all were, the adults, me, Connor, even the fish. My eyes popped open.

I had solved the case!

Chapter Nine

I told Connor what I thought. He nodded, serious-like, and said, "I think you're right."

So I went to Halmoni and whispered what I knew. "What should we do now?"

"Let's wait for the officer to arrive," she said. "Then we'll tell her and the Lees at the same time."

A couple of minutes later Officer Duong came in. She went over to Mr. and Mrs. Lee.

Halmoni, Connor and I followed, and I told them what I thought.

They listened.

Officer Duong went to the fish tank and used the strainer to turn over the stones. I felt the butterflies in my stomach. We had looked for the diamonds in front of the tank, behind it and under it too. But we hadn't looked *in* the tank. I tried to calm the butterflies as Officer Duong searched. After a few seconds, she smiled and lifted the strainer out of the water. "Lark, open your hand."

I did, and she gently shook out the strainer. The diamond earrings fell into my palm. Officer Duong turned to the group of grown-ups. "Henry, is there something you want to say?"

His eyes went wide. "You think I did it?"

Connor and I nodded.

Henry's face went growly. "I didn't take them. You can't prove anything!"

"Lark's holding the earrings right now."

"So?" he said. "Anybody could've put them in the tank."

"It had to be you," I said, "because your words gave you away."

Everyone turned to look at Henry.

He gulped.

"Lark," said Mrs. Wiedman, "why do you think it's Henry?"

"Because of the fish," I said. "Dad says when it comes to feeding them, you have to be very responsible. They can only be fed once a day, and then only a certain amount. The Lees always feed the fish at eight in the morning. But we got here at ten. I know because Connor and I were sad we'd missed giving them breakfast. They shouldn't have been hungry, so it made me wonder why Henry said they looked hungry. Plus, he said he fed them again," I continued. "That's when I realized that maybe Henry had taken the earrings." I looked at him. "But you had to hide them quickly—"

"Mrs. Lee glanced over, and I got scared," he said. "I was worried that she'd seen me take the earrings. I pretended to feed the fish, but really I was dropping the earrings in the tank. I thought I'd get them later, when everyone was gone and the store was quiet."

"The diamonds are clear, so they blended in with the pebbles," said Connor. "It was a good hiding place." He grinned. "Until Lark figured it out."

"We did it together," I told him. "When you talked about food, I remembered about Henry feeding the fish."

"I'm sorry, Mr. and Mrs. Lee," Henry said glumly. "But I needed the money for my car."

Both the Lees looked really sad.

"If you had just told us," said Mrs. Lee, "we would have lent you the money."

"Instead, you're coming with me to the police station. Come on. Let's go," said Officer Duong. She led Henry out the door to her police car.

Chapter Ten

Mr. Lee came over to us. "That was great detective work! I'm very impressed! Thank you for helping us." He held the detective poster that Conner had been making notes on. "I'm going to put this right beside the cash register, and I'm going to tell everyone what you did!"

Connor grinned.

I grinned even bigger. "Thank you!"

Mrs. Lee gave both of us a giant hug and handed us each a dollar. "And for the rest of the summer, you can have a free Popsicle every day!"

Wow! This was the *bestest* day ever!

"That's so great, Mrs. Lee. Thank you," said Connor.

"Thank you again," said Mrs. Lee. "I'm just tickled pink that we got our jewelry back!" She gave me another hug.

I didn't understand. I knew neither Connor or I had tickled Mrs. Lee.

Plus, she didn't look pink. But she was smiling at me, so I smiled back.

Even though we had solved the case, there was something we still had to do. Only we had to wait until the sun set before we could do it.

Chapter Eleven

I knocked on Sophie's door.

Sophie opened it. "I didn't think you were going to show up. It's getting late."

"We had to wait until it was darker if we were going to help with the monster movie," said Connor.

I was holding a bottle.

Sophie looked at it. "I already tried soda." She looked at the light in Connor's hand. "What's that for? We already have lights for shooting the movie when it's dark outside."

"This one is special, and it's better for the monster experiment."

She shrugged. "Ma, I'm in the backyard with the sheep people!"

Connor growled. "Totally not cool."

"She's just joking," I said. "Best friends like us joke all the time."

We went into the backyard. Sophie got an extension cord and plugged in our light.

"It's a black light," said Connor. "It shows when stuff glows in the dark."

Sophie frowned.

"And this is tonic water. It has a special ingredient called quinine that's going to make the soda glow in the dark. Trust me. It's going to work. We read about it in a science book we borrowed from the library yesterday."

We took the label off the bottle so we could see inside it. Then we rolled up a piece of paper so we could use it as a tube to hold the mints. Once everything was set up, Sophie's mom came out to make sure everything was safe. She stood to the side and started recording. "Ready? Go!"

Connor used the tube to drop a bunch of mints into the bottle, then ran away as it sank to the bottom. Almost immediately there was a huge gush of water that glowed blue in the light.

We all cheered and clapped our hands. Sophie cheered the loudest! "This is amazing! It really is superduper cool! It's perfect for the monster movie!" She smiled at me. "Thanks, Lark sheep!"

I felt great. I had found the stolen earrings and figured out how the culprit

had hidden them. Plus, I had helped
Sophie make an awesome explosion.
I was a really amazing, excellent P.I.

Chapter Twelve

"Come on! Come on!" I bounced on the chair and waited for family talent night to start.

"Be patient," said Mom. "We're coming!"

When everyone got settled, the evening began. Mom showed off her amazing memory by reciting a really long poem about a road that split into two paths in a wood. It was kind of a boring poem, but the adults all cheered and said stuff like, "It's so moving! What a great poem!" So I clapped and cheered and said, "It's the best poem ever," because I wanted my mom to feel good about her talent. Dad and Max danced the cha-cha. Max was much better at it than Dad was, but I didn't say anything.

Halmoni stood. "My talent is the inside-out-upside-down-make-your-tummy-flip cake."

Cake!

Connor jumped up and gave everyone a plate and fork.

Halmoni put the cake on the table. "It's a special cake. It's solid on the outside, but on the inside is a chocolate river."

Connor frowned. So did I.

"If the cake is cooked, then it's all solid," he said.

"Behold!" Halmoni cut the cake, and a river of chocolate ran out!

"Wow," said Connor. "That's amazing!"

I was too busy helping eat the cake to say anything. Besides, it would have been rude to talk with my mouth full. So I smiled and kept eating. I only wanted one piece, but I also wanted to make Halmoni feel good about baking a delicious, spicy, yummy chocolate cake. So I had three pieces. I would have had four, but Mom made a frowny face at me.

"What's your magical talent?" Mom asked us when we'd finished eating.

"Watch!" I gave Halmoni a quick hug of thanks, then ran to stand by Connor. We'd practiced the disappearing-coin trick, but then we decided to do something else. Something that would be amazing and make Halmoni very happy.

"This is an ordinary star." Connor held up a star he'd cut out of yellow paper. "But with a little spell, it becomes magic. It will change its appearance as it travels through the air, unseen, to land at a new location!" He held the star in the palm of his hand.

I waved a piece of red velvet cloth in front of him. "Abracadabra, ala-ka-honi!" I dropped the cloth over the star. "Travel, star, to our halmoni!" As I pulled the cloth back up I secretly grabbed one of the star's points in Connor's hand. It looked like the star had disappeared, but it was hidden in the velvet cloth.

Connor held up his hands to show they were empty.

Mom, Dad and Halmoni oohed and aahed.

"We're not done yet," I said. "Halmoni, reach into your pocket."

She did, and her eyes widened as she pulled out a yellow star. "Oh, my goodness!"

"It's no ordinary star," said Connor as he went over to her. "Look, we decorated it."

"Yes," said Halmoni, "I see the gold glitter." She squinted. "Are those lima beans glued to the edges?"

I nodded. "You helped us solve the case. Without you, I'm not sure we would have gotten all the clues we needed to make Henry spill the beans."

"You deserve a gold star," said Connor, "because you're a very big help to us P.I.s."

Mom and Dad whispered. Then Dad stood.

"The judges have conferred, and we have a tie," he said. "Connor and Lark, you win our family talent night, and Halmoni wins too"—he smiled—"for her help in solving the case and because this cake is delicious."

"We win!" Connor jumped up and down.

"Yes," said Mom. "But I get a special mention because I'm about to perform a second, astounding magic trick."

"What are you going to do?" I asked.

She grabbed the plate with the rest of the cake. "I'm going to make this cake disappear!" Then she started eating it.

She laughed, and we did too. Mom put the plate down and cut pieces for each of us.

"Connor," I said. "We solved a case, we helped Sophie and we won family talent night. Today really is the bestest day ever."

THE WORDS LARK LOVES

CHAPTER THREE:

I really liked this idea, and Halmoni's plan. It made me think of a word, but I couldn't remember it. It started with a p, *and it had an* o *in it, and it was a good word.*

The word Lark was thinking of was *proactive.* It's an awesome word! It means rather than waiting for good things to happen to them, Lark and Connor go out and make good things happen. Instead of waiting for Halmoni or Mom or Dad to tell them there's a case, Lark and Connor check their mailbox and emails to find out for themselves.

CHAPTER EIGHT:

I nodded. "Yep, yep, you don't have to be—" I couldn't remember the word, but it was a good one, and it had a great oo sound. It meant when you were so sad it was like rain clouds were over your head.

Lark knew the definition but not the word. That amazing word is *gloomy*. If you are ever feeling extra sad, you could be feeling gloomy.

THE STUFF LARK
ALMOST GOT RIGHT

CHAPTER THREE:

When Halmoni left the kitchen, Connor turned to me. His face had lots of worried squiggles. "I don't know if I can be on a ball," he said.

"Me either," I said. "Cutting paper and drawing might be hard if we have to sit on Mom and Dad's yoga balls to do it."

Being *on the ball* doesn't mean sitting on a ball. It's a fun way to say you pay attention to what's happening around you, and if something needs to be done, you act right away. For example, when Lark and Connor didn't wake up to any cases, instead of being sad, they made posters to let people know they were private investigators looking for cases.

CHAPTER TEN:

"Thank you again," said Mrs. Lee. "I'm just tickled pink that we got our jewelry back!" She gave me another hug.

I didn't understand. I knew neither Connor or I had tickled Mrs. Lee. Plus, she didn't look pink.

Tickled pink is a saying that's been around for a really long time. It means to be extra, extra happy that something good has happened to you. For example, if you end up being the first one on the playground and you get the swings, you might be tickled pink at your luck!

Award-winning author **NATASHA DEEN** graduated from the University of Alberta with a BA in psychology. In addition to her work as a presenter and workshop facilitator with schools, she writes for kids, young adults and adults. Natasha was the 2013 Regional Writer in Residence for the Metro Edmonton Library Federation. Natasha lives in Edmonton, Alberta. For more information, please visit her website at www.natashadeen.com.